P.K. HALLINAN

A Rainbow of Friends

For my rainbow of friends—
the children of this earth.

Ideals Children's Books
Nashville, Tennessee
an imprint of Hambleton-Hill Publishing, Inc.

Published by Ideals Children's Books
An imprint of Hambleton-Hill Publishing, Inc.
Nashville, Tennessee 37218

Printed and bound in the United States of America

Library of Congress Cataloging-in-Publication Data
Hallinan, P.K.
    A rainbow of friends / written and illustrated by P.K. Hallinan.
        p.   cm.
    Summary: A story in verse about how all friends are special and
valuable regardless of differences or difficulties.
    ISBN 1-57102-104-3 (rev. pbk. edition)—ISBN 0-8249-8657-1 (lib.)
    [1. Friendship—Fiction. 2. Multiculturalism—Fiction. 3. Stories
in rhyme.] I. Title.
    PZ8.3.H15Ra1   1994
    [E]—dc20   93-39257
                                                             CIP
                                                             AC

A rainbow of friends
is the vision we see
when we think about peace
and world harmony.

Some friends are funny.

Some friends are stars.

Some friends wear clothing
that's different from ours.

But all friends are special
and add in some way
to the richness of life—
how we think, what we say.

A rainbow of friends
is a dream we can share
where everyone's treated
with kindness and care.

A friend may be challenged
in movement or speech.

A friend may be distant
or difficult to reach.

Still, each friend is given
a share of our hearts,
so no one feels different,
unloved, or apart.

A rainbow of friends
is a chance for us all
to help one another
when we stumble or fall.

We all have our interests.

We all have our views.

We all have our strengths
and our weaknesses too.

And though we may wander
a bit wide or far,
our friends still accept us
the way that we are.

A rainbow of friends
is a bonding together
that eases our journey
through all kinds of weather.

If we work hand in hand,
all jobs can be done.

If we play as a team,
we've already won.

Our goals can be reached with the greatest success by trusting that others are doing their best.

So reach out with love
to the people you meet,
and offer a smile
to all those you greet.

The world is a family
whose happiness depends
on a circle of caring . . .

on a rainbow of friends.